This book is dedicated to the memory of my
un-born son, Michael Grant Fetters.

It was the encouragement of my wife
Sharol Lynn who kept after me to
make Horace come alive for our son
and the future we were never to share.

Mike, Sharol, I hope you like it.

Grant Fetters

Horace the Hopper

This is the story of Horace. Horace is a small green Grasshopper. He lives in a little grassy spot near the woods on the outskirts of town. Horace has many friends: Bert the Beetle, Lois the Ladybug, Steve the Spider, and Fred the Fly.

Horace and his friends would play all day long. They would play "hop each other" or "hide and seek." Sometimes they would just sit and talk. They were the best of friends.

One day, Horace was resting in the shade with his friends. Nearby there were some Ants working. All the Ants were so very busy. Horace was thinking, "*They just keep on working. Those ants never have any fun. They are always working.*"

Horace and his friends were all sitting and watching the clouds go floating bye.

Horace noticed something sticking just above the trees in the distance.

"What is that?" asked Horace, "above the trees?"

Bert the Beetle said, "Oh, that's the town's building tops."

"Oooh, what's a town?" asked Horace.

"That is where the people live," said Bert. "They have homes, schools, children, and they also have CARS."

"What's a CAR?" exclaimed Horace.

"You don't need to know that," Lois said. "All you need to know, is that YOU NEED to stay clear of them. They are nothing but trouble."

"But, what are they?" asked Horace.

"I am not sure," said Steve. "All I know, is that they are very big and they will squish you if you get in the way."

"I want to go to town," said Horace.

"I want to see what goes on there. I want to see the people, the children and the cars. Bert, do you know how to get to the town?"

"No, Horace, I am not sure," said Bert. "I have never been there."

Steve jumped up and said, "It is such a very long distance, it would take you forever to get there."

"It would not be so far," Lois said, "if you had help getting there."

"So how do I get there?" asked Horace? "I want to go exploring. I want to see what I am missing. I need help."

"There is someone that might be able to help," said Bert.

"Who?" asked Horace?

"The Owl," said Bert. "The Owl knows everything."

"Yes," said Lois. "That's right, the Owl can help. If anyone would know how you can get to the town, it would be the Owl."

"If you must go?" said Steve, "I think you should go see the Owl. He is very smart. He will put you on the right path."

"That's what I am going to do," said Horace. "I'm going to find the Owl."

So Horace headed off into the woods in search of the Owl.

At each tree, Horace would look up into the tree and call out. "Owl! Owl! Are you up there? I need your help." Horace searched for hours until dark when the Owl woke up and could hear Horace calling for him.

"Yes!" said the Owl. "Who is that? Who is calling for me?"

"It is me, Horace."

"What do you want of me?" asked the Owl.

Horace cried up, "I need your help. I want to go to the town. I want to explore the world. I want to see things that I've never..."

"Wait, wait just a minute!" shouted the Owl. "Start at the top. What is this all about?"

"I want to go to the town and see the people, the children, the homes, and the CARS!" said Horace.

"Oh, what a foolish Grass-Hopper," said the Owl. "What do you know about these things?"

"That's the point," said Horace. "I want to experience new things. I want to see unusual sights."

"You have all you should ever want or need right here in the grassy spot where you live," said Owl. "You have many friends, and you have nothing to worry about, except where to play."

"But Owl," cried Horace. "I need to do this. Will you help me? Can you tell me how I can get to the town?"

"Yes, I will help you," said Owl. "But I want you to know this. I think that you are making a big mistake."

So The Owl swooped down and picked up Horace and carried him up to the very top of the largest tree in the forest. At that point Horace could see the town's lights. "*Oh what a beautiful sight,*" Horace was thinking. As the Owl and Horace sat at the top of the tree, Horace thought of all the exciting things he would experience, and that made him want to go all that much more.

"Now Horace," said Owl. "You must be very careful. There are things that you do not know or understand out there. You will experience many new and unusual things. And you will also be in great danger."

"Danger," scoffed Horace. "What could possibly hurt me?"

“Do not trust the people,” warned the Owl. “They will catch you and you will end up in a jar, or worse. You'll be looking through the glass of a very small world. And that is where you will stay.”

“Oh, don't worry about me. I'll be all right,” said Horace. “So let's get started. How do I get there?”

As the sun was coming up, Horace and the Owl were perched on top of the tree, watching the morning sun rise. They sat there for a minute and looked towards the town.

The Owl started to give his instructions. "You must wait for a big gust of wind to

come along. At that point you just jump off the tree and let the wind carry you towards the town. You'll be there before you know it. I'll tell you when to jump."

"Well that seems easy...." said Horace.

"Now!!" yelled the Owl.

"I'll be back!!" said Horace.

"Not right away!" said the Owl. "Good Luck."

Well Horace took off like a shot. He flew and he flew.

Horace was soaring like the mighty Eagle. He was getting the ride of his life.

Horace could see the town getting closer and closer, when all of a sudden there was a quick down draft and Horace was falling like a rock.

"Oh nooo!" said Horace. "What am I going to do?"

Horace felt something grab him by the leg. Horace was being carried off to a nest by a Robin. Horace did not want to be the main course back at the Robin's home so he spoke up.

"Excuse me, Mrs. Robin." As Horace spoke, the Robin, who did not know Grass Hoppers could talk, let Horace go. So then Horace fell softly to the ground.

"*Wow!*" thought Horace. "*This is great! I made it! So this is what a town is.*" Horace was standing on the sidewalk in the middle of town. He was so excited about being in a different place other than the grassy spot where he grew up, back home.

As he started to look around there was this loud bell ringing and a very large wheel came within a few, "grasshopper" inches. Horace jumped onto the grass next to the sidewalk.

"That was close!" Horace thought. *"I must be more careful."*

Horace decided it was time to see the town and explore new and exciting things.

Horace saw the children playing at the school. There were people walking down the streets.

The street that Horace was on had homes, stores, and cars that zoomed by right in front of him. Horace wanted to get closer to the children across the street at the playground. They were jumping and running and having a great time. So Horace headed off across the street. The street was wide and there were plenty of cars in the street. Horace had to dodge the cars to get across the street. They were very large and moved very fast.

Horace saw his chance, so he hopped like crazy and soon he made it to the other side.

"Wow!" said Horace. "That was scary. Cars are nothing to fool with."

Horace was standing by the fence, watching the children play.

"Those children are having so much fun," Horace thought. *"I wish I could play with them. I want to play with them. What could it hurt?"*

Horace had forgotten all the instructions of the Owl and the advice of his friends back home. All Horace knew was that he was on a great adventure, and nothing was going to stop him. So Horace hopped out to where the children were playing. One of the little boys spotted Horace and he reached down and grabbed Horace and squeezed him in his hand.

The next thing Horace knew, he was tossed in a jar with some grass and a stick.

"What is going on here?" Horace chirped. "Where am I? What's the big idea?"

Horace had been tossed in an old mason jar, and then he was placed on the counter in the classroom. The little boy who had picked Horace up had captured him and had locked him away in a jar.

"Oh no!" Horace cried. "What will I do now? I know, I'll just jump out and away I'll go."

So Horace jumped and he jumped and he jumped. There was netting blocking the opening to the jar and he was trapped.

No matter how hard he tried to jump out of the jar, Horace could not get past the netting.

Horace could see through the glass. He could also see there were many children in the classroom where he was placed.

"*Now I've really done it this time,*" Horace thought. "*How am I ever going to get out of this mess?*"

Every day the children would come over to the jar where Horace was, and they would each take turns holding the jar.

They would roll it, and shake it, and make poor old Horace very dizzy.

This activity went on for many days. Horace did not have much choice in this. There was little he could do to change things. He sat down and thought, "*Am I going to be trapped in this jar for the rest of my life?*" Horace would catch himself thinking about the friends back home in the grassy spot near the woods. He was wishing he were back home and not stuck in the jar. But all he could do was dream. Horace would dream about the good times he had back home.

Then one day, just like all the others, the children came to look at Horace in the jar. They started to toss Horace and the jar around in the classroom.

Then "CRASH!!" The jar fell to the counter, and the glass broke. Horace could see his chance.

"I've got to go!" said Horace. "I have to get out of here! I'm going home!"

Horace hopped and he hopped, and he finally made it to the window. The window was open and Horace hopped out the window and away he went. Horace hopped so much that his legs grew very tired. It was getting dark and Horace had a very long way to go to get

home. So Horace stopped for the night and rested.

The next day Horace woke up to hear some familiar sound.

"What was that?" Horace thought. *"I've heard those voices before. That sounds like Bert."*

Horace hopped up on top of a rock so he could see farther. He could not see

anything that looked like home but he could hear the voices that sounded so familiar. Horace moved closer and closer to the sound. All of a sudden he broke through the brush and could see. Yes indeed, he was home and all of his friends were there playing in the grass. So Horace hopped
over to them and surprised them.

"Horace! Horace!" Bert yelled. "Where have you been? We have been worried sick about you. We thought you were squished by a car or something."
"Yeah," said Steve. "Where have you been?"

"I am so glad you are back, safe and sound." said Lois.

Horace was so very glad to be finally home with his friends. He could not control himself.

"Boy-o-boy do I have a story to tell you." said Horace. "I have seen the world, and what a frightening place it is. There are many great and wonderful things. I've seen many items that I did not understand and they were very scary. I would not trade them for anything. Nor would I like to re-live some of them. Well guys, I am so glad to be home. Lets all go play." "Ok, Horace, let's go." said Bert. "It's good to have you home."

Made in the USA
Charleston, SC
20 August 2011